Life Under the Sea

# Squids

by Mari Schuh

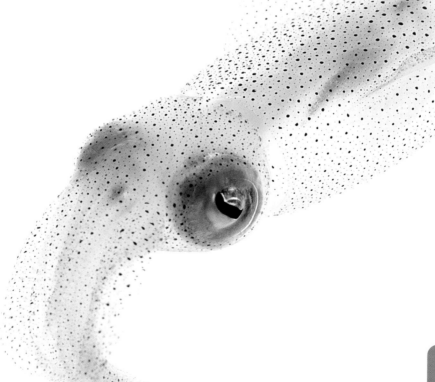

Bullfrog
Books

# Ideas for Parents and Teachers

Bullfrog Books let children practice reading informational text at the earliest reading levels. Repetition, familiar words, and photo labels support early readers.

## Before Reading

· Discuss the cover photo. What does it tell them?

· Look at the picture glossary together. Read and discuss the words.

## Read the Book

· "Walk" through the book and look at the photos. Let the child ask questions. Point out the photo labels.

· Read the book to the child, or have him or her read independently.

## After Reading

· Prompt the child to think more. Ask: Have you ever seen a squid? Was it swimming?

Bullfrog Books are published by Jump!
5357 Penn Avenue South
Minneapolis, MN 55419
www.jumplibrary.com

Library of Congress Cataloging-in-Publication Data

Schuh, Mari C., 1975- author.
 Squids / by Mari Schuh.
  pages cm. — (Life under the sea)
 "Bullfrog Books are published by Jump!"
 Summary: "This photo-illustrated book for beginning readers describes the physical features and behaviors of squids. Includes picture glossary and index"—Provided by publisher.
 Audience: 5-8.
 Audience: K to grade 3.
 Includes index.
 ISBN 978-1-62031-193-6 (hardcover: alk. paper) — ISBN 978-1-62496-280-6 (ebook)
 1. Squids—Juvenile literature. 1. Title.
 II. Series: Bullfrog books. Life under the sea.
 QL430.2.S38 2016
 594.58—dc23
                                    2014043357

Editor: Jenny Fretland VanVoorst
Series Designer: Ellen Huber
Book Designer: Michelle Sonnek
Photo Researcher: Michelle Sonnek

Photo Credits: age fotostock, 24; Alamy, 15; Biosphoto, 20-21; Getty, 4, 17; Nature Picture Library, cover, 3; Science Source Images, 10-11; Shutterstock, 4, 8-9, 12, 14-15, 18-19, 22; SuperStock, 5, 6-7, 14-15, 16, 18-19; Thinkstock, 1, 13.

Printed in the United States of America at Corporate Graphics in North Mankato, Minnesota.

For my brother John—MS

# Table of Contents

A squid swims in the sea.

He hunts for prey.

funnel

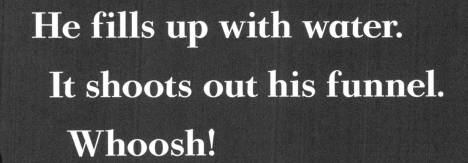

He fills up with water.

It shoots out his funnel.

Whoosh!

He jets away.
He is big.
But he is fast!

He can change
his color.

It helps him hide.

# Look! A fish!

The squid grabs it.
He uses his tentacles.
They are long.

tentacle

He eats his meal.

He uses his beak.

Yum!

beak

**Oh no! A seal!**

It's okay.
The squid has a plan.

He squirts dark ink.

It is cloudy.

The seal is dazed.

ink

Time to go!
The squid swims away.
He hides in the
dark sea.

21

# Parts of a Squid

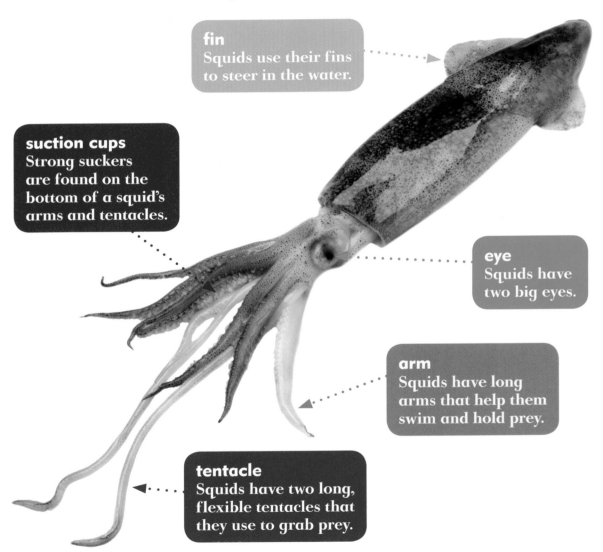

**fin**
Squids use their fins to steer in the water.

**suction cups**
Strong suckers are found on the bottom of a squid's arms and tentacles.

**eye**
Squids have two big eyes.

**arm**
Squids have long arms that help them swim and hold prey.

**tentacle**
Squids have two long, flexible tentacles that they use to grab prey.

# Picture Glossary

**beak**
The hard part of a squid's mouth on the underside of its body.

**ink**
Dark liquid that a squid squirts out when in danger.

**hunt**
To look for animals to eat.

**prey**
Animals that are hunted for food.

# Index

# To Learn More

Learning more is as easy as 1, 2, 3.

1) Go to www.factsurfer.com

2) Enter "squids" into the search box.

3) Click the "Surf" button to see a list of websites.

With factsurfer.com, finding more information is just a click away.

24